Let It Be

(A Sometimes Never novella)

By Cheryl McIntyre

Let It Be (A Sometimes Never Novella)

Cheryl McIntyre

Copyright Cheryl McIntyre 2014

Published at Smashwords

Cover photo by Scott Hoover—Courtesy of Love N. Books

Cover model Jacob Sones

Cover design by Sommer Stein

Edited by Dawn McIntyre Decker

August 2014

Table of Contents

Prologue

Guy

I would like to say I've always known exactly who I am.

I'd like to tell you that I somehow skipped over the confusion and struggles with my self-esteem, self-worth, self-image. I'd like to say I have always accepted myself and my sexuality.

That I grew up gay and proud.

I'd like to say that, but it would be a lie.

At eleven years old, when most of the kids in my school were showing interest in the opposite sex, I was absorbed in music and video games. And I saw nothing wrong with that. In fact, I paid absolutely no attention to it at all.

And then one day, right around my twelfth birthday, it happened. Troy Jensen transferred to my school. He walked into my band class. Our gazes met as Mrs. Farrow introduced him, and I thought he had the nicest smile I had ever seen. His eyes were like green glass and they held me captive.

I tried to stop staring because I didn't want him to think I was weird, but the more I looked at him, the less I wanted to look away. He was the first person I ever thought was beautiful. Not pretty. Not cute. Not glamorous or interesting.

He was *beautiful*.

I'd like to say it hit me like an epiphany. That the clouds parted and the sun shone down on me with a sudden clarity as trumpets played the sweetest symphony. That I realized I was gay. And I was okay with it.

I'd like to say that—I really wish I could—but it would be a lie.

No matter how incredibly right it felt, it just felt wrong.

I felt wrong.

So I fought against it. I tried to *ignore it*. I *hid it* from everyone. Especially Troy Jensen. The more my friends talked about girls, the more I tried to embrace heterosexuality. I joined in the discussions about girls—who was the prettiest, who I wanted to get to which base with, who was most likely to allow me to get to those bases, and so on.

But the whole time, I knew it was a lie.

I didn't want it to be untrue. I tried to *force* myself to actually feel the way I was pretending to feel. Claiming to feel. *Begging* to feel.

But I couldn't do it.

No matter how hard I tried, no matter how hard I fought—and against everything I was raised to believe—I couldn't hide from the fact that I was different.

I liked boys.

I liked boys the way my friends liked girls.

And so, one day, I started using my closet for what it was really meant for—clothes and shoes, and random shit you can't find a place for—and I stepped out. Because I wasn't some random thing that didn't have a place.

I was a person who just wanted one thing out of my life. The same thing *everyone, everywhere* wants.

Happiness.

And you can't be happy living a lie.

I decided being different was a blessing—not a mistake, not a curse, not a disease. And I had every right to that happiness as everyone else.

Unfortunately for me, I didn't understand what true happiness was until it was taken away.

One

Guy

I don't know exactly when it all went wrong. Maybe I *should* know. Maybe that was the problem. But I didn't have a clue. Looking back, I realize there were signs. Nothing big or glaring, but signs all the same. If I only understood what I was looking at.

When Ian frowned, I would tickle him until he laughed. When he refused to get out of bed, I would lay in bed with him, vegging out and watching TV alongside of him. When he refused to go out with me because he was tired or sick for the fourth time that week, I would bug him, making him feel guilty until I either got my way or gave up. And when he would pick fights with me over random nothingness, it eventually got to me, and I would tell him he was crazy.

I close my eyes, trying to keep the tears from falling.

I told him he was crazy.

It must have killed him a little more each time I said it. How could I do that? How could I have said that to him? What kind of person does that?

I'm so selfish. I always made it all about me. What I wanted. What I needed. We argued so much. The fact that he wanted to hide our relationship hurt so badly at the time. I threw ultimatums and accusations left and right.

It's all so meaningless now.

So pointless.

My fingers curl around his hand lying beside him, limp and cool in the hospital bed. I don't touch the bandage on his wrist, afraid it will start to bleed again if I make contact with it.

The image of him, floating in a bath of his own blood is burned into my mind forever. I'll never forget. It will never go away.

Nothing will ever be the same.

The door opens and I release his hand immediately. The nurse smiles gently at me after she injects something into Ian's IV. I think she knows who I really am, though I haven't offered her that information. For now, I'll continue to play the role of concerned roommate.

"He's doing well," she says softly. "His stats are good. Blood pressure is exactly where we want to see it."

I nod, staying quiet. I think if I allow myself to talk right now—even something as little as a thank you—I'll burst into tears, sobbing beside my unconscious boyfriend. That isn't what he needs. It's not what he would want.

I have to be strong. For him.

The rock, the pillar, the anchor—that's my job.

"Talk to him," the nurse adds. "Sometimes it helps."

My blurry eyes follow her until she crosses the threshold, leaving the room.

Sometimes it helps.

I wonder if she means for him or me.

I drag the chair over to his bed and lower myself heavily. I feel like I've aged ten years. Every muscle aches— weighed down from the heaviness I carry in my heart. My hands are shaking as I grasp the railing, pressing my forehead to it. And then I talk.

"We met on a Friday. I know, because that's the day I always used to stop in Marlow's Music. Every Friday, like clockwork, to browse the half-priced CDs, though I rarely ever bought.

"Our hands met as we both reached for a Misfits album—ironic, I know. It was like an electric shock—sparks dancing along all five fingers and absorbing in my palm. Though you've never said it, I think you felt it too. You looked at me and I'll never forget the way you smiled. Uninhibited and carefree. You took my breath away in that moment. And I knew I needed to know you. You didn't pull your hand away, so neither did I.

"Instead, you bent your head toward me and asked, 'Did you know this store is named after a dog? Because I didn't. I've been calling the old lady behind the counter Marlow for weeks. I couldn't understand why she kept giving me the evil eye until she finally snapped at me today. Marlow was actually her husband's dog. Apparently it's a touchy subject—her husband naming their store after a dog as opposed to her—but I kind of get why.'

"We both turned then, glancing back at the old woman behind the counter. She glared at us and we burst into shameless laughter. We spent the next hour talking as we walked aimlessly around the small store. You bought the Misfits album and insisted I take it. And when I got home, I found your number scrawled across the label. Such a brazen move on your part, but really I had the hardest task—making the call and asking you out.

"We were inseparable from that moment on.

"I never told you this, but I noticed you immediately when I walked through the door that day, skipping your fingers along a stack of records. Something about you wouldn't let me look away. You were captivating with your messy dark hair and soft blue eyes. The most fascinating person I ever laid eyes on.

"I think you stole a piece of my heart within those first few seconds. You took it and you never gave it back.

"But that's okay. I don't want it back. It's yours to keep, and there's so much more waiting here for you when you wake up.

"Because you have to wake up, Ian. You *have* to.

"You have to.

"*You have to.*

"We'll do everything your way, I promise. On your terms. However you want it. I'll never complain again. Just. Wake. *Up*.

"*Please*. I don't know who I am without you."

Two

Ian

"When I was little, I thought I was a superhero," Guy says out of nowhere.

"Which one?" I hold my hand up, stopping him before he can begin. "Hold on, let me guess. Batman. No. He's too dark and...*throaty*. The Flash? No, Superman."

His lips twitch with amusement. "Batarangs and speed have never been my thing, but I've always wanted to fly. And being bulletproof? Come on. Fan-fucking-tastic."

"I KNEW IT." I let my smile drop, looking at him seriously. "I can see it. You have that hero vibe about you."

"What? Sexy, smart, and addictively charming? That's just good genes."

"Don't forget modest," I add with a smirk.

He laughs, the sound more than appealing. "No point in hiding what's so blaringly obvious."

Now I laugh. I like this guy. Ha—*this Guy*. A lot.

I've never felt like this before. This frenzied rush of adrenaline, anxiety, attraction, and joy. It's too much all at once. But it's the best thing I've ever experienced in my life.

I'm on cloud fucking nine. And ten. And elven. And twelve.

Chinese food has never tasted better in all my twenty-three years than it does at this very second. It's a scrumptious work of art. I want to share it with the world even though I know they won't understand.

I click a picture and upload it to Facebook with the caption: *Best Lo Mein of my life.*

Questions pop up instantly, wanting to know where I am. I ignore them, slipping my phone back into my pocket because it has nothing to do with the place. It's all about my current company. Like I said—they won't understand.

"You're smiling a lot over there," Guy says. He shoves his chopsticks into his container of rice, giving me his full attention, which I can't get enough of. "Care to share what has you in such a good mood?"

I grin around a mouthful of noodles, offering him a wink. "Nope." I don't think I really need to tell him. I think he knows he's responsible for my bliss.

"Hm," Guy grunts. "I hope it just has more to do with me and less to do with the food. Did I see you snap a picture?"

I nod, swallowing my bite. "For Facebook. I might not be able to post a pic of us or announce we're on our first date, but I can share a photo of our meal. We'll know what I really mean. That's better anyway—like our own little secret."

His brows furrow, unpleased, casting a shadow over his eyes. "I don't know how I feel about being a secret," he utters.

And just like that, my good mood pops like overinflated balloon. "It won't be forever," I murmur. "I just need some time."

Three

Guy

"Did I ever tell you how Hope and I met? I can't remember." I pause, though I know he can't hear me.

"It was at my Uncle Donnie's funeral—one of the four worst days of my life.

"I'm sure you can guess this day is at the very top of that list, now replacing the day my mom left.

"Anyway...I trailed behind my dad with my head cast down. I didn't want to be there. In fact, I would have paid to be anywhere else but there.

"All the people made me uncomfortable. I didn't know any of them. Outside of my family, the only person I knew was lying in one of the coffins in the front of the room.

"Is that the right word?

"Coffin?

"It feels wrong somehow. Like Uncle Donnie was a

vampire, ready to rise at dusk to suck the blood of the innocent." I chuckle lightly. Laughing is the last thing I feel like doing right now, but I can't help finding the terrible irony—talking to Ian about death, coffins, and funerals while he lies in a hospital bed, fighting for his life.

Hell, I don't even know if he's fighting.

I clear my throat and keep going.

"A flash of color caught my eye. I glanced over and noticed a young girl with multi-colored hair. She was so small and cute, like I could tuck her into my pocket. But her eyes were the saddest things I had ever seen. I couldn't stop staring at her and I'm not sure why.

"Maybe it was because she was subtly falling back, letting the crowd hide her from the double coffins in the front of the room.

"And then I realized who she was.

"I glanced over at the long, dark hair of Uncle Donnie's girlfriend lying motionless in her satin bed.

"Then my gaze slid back to the girl and I realized she was the one that would be my new foster sister.

"Someone up front made an announcement and the crowd thinned as people found seats. I tugged the sleeves of my two-sizes-too-small suit—you would have loved it, Ian, it was completely ridiculous—and that's when she noticed me. I watched her as she took in my dumbass outfit.

"And then she laughed, one of those surprised snorts she does—you know what I'm talking about. It was so loud in the otherwise quiet room. Heads turned in her direction, making her blush. And you know Hope doesn't blush easily.

"I felt like total shit for making her laugh at a funeral—her *mom's* funeral. So I smiled back apologetically. I wiggled the knot on my hot pink tie—you would have loved the tie, too. I might still have it over at my dad's house somewhere. I'll have to look.

"Anyway, Dad nudged me into the chair then, right next to some old woman I guess I was—am—apparently related to, and I lost sight of Hope.

"My dad leaned into me and whispered, 'I hate these things.'

"I just raised a brow, because seriously, doesn't everybody? I never met a person who told me they loved attending funerals.

"'I never know what to say,' he continued. 'Everybody always says they're sorry. But what are they sorry for?'

"I shrugged, and you know what I said to him?" I pause again, giving him the chance to answer me, but of course, he doesn't.

"'Maybe they're sorry for being happy it isn't them that died.'

"I actually said that. And at the time, I believed it."

I suck in a harsh breath, my lungs trembling beneath my ribcage.

"I don't feel that way anymore, Ian. I swear, I don't.

I'd trade places with you in a heartbeat if only it were possible."

When the tears clear my vision, I sweep the hair off of his head, letting my fingers soak in the texture of each strand. Ian's always had the softest, smoothest hair.

I take another long breath and keep going.

"Some...someone was talking about Uncle Donnie and how they met when I spotted Hope again. She was sitting by herself in the very back. Family was supposed to sit up front, but I think she knew that. She just didn't care.

"I told Dad I was going to go sit with her because nobody should sit alone at their mom's funeral.

"Dad looked at her for a long moment and then turned back to me. He just nodded me on. I think he could see she was broken just as easily as I could.

"Hope's head lifted when I slid in next to her. I whispered a hello. I knew I shouldn't talk to her during the funeral, but I got the impression she wasn't paying attention to the eulogy anyway.

"I told her my name. She knew that already too, but you know how I am when I meet someone new.

"She smiled as she pushed a chunk of rainbow hair behind her ear—did you know she used to dye her hair? Exactly like a rainbow. I'll have to show you pictures when you wake up. It was really unique. Different. You would have thought it was beautiful.

"Anyway, I didn't tell her I was sorry about her mom. She didn't tell me she was sorry about my uncle. Instead, she inclined closer to me and extended an ear bud." I smile again with the memory. "I had to stifle a laugh because I realized she had been listening to music the entire time. It was The Cure. So inappropriately appropriate.

"After the funeral, everybody came back to our house.

"You know, I've never really understood that part. How does standing around with a bunch of strangers, shoving food in our mouths, help the grieving process? As if the unknown casseroles and ridiculous array of desserts will somehow magically make me miss my loved one less.

"It doesn't.

"It's a stupid ritual.

"But I filled a plate to overflowing anyway, and shoved a couple of bottles of water into my pockets to take up to Hope in the tree house. As soon as she spotted it when we got home, she headed straight for it.

"I elbowed the door in the floor open and my eyes met hers. I think she had been crying, or maybe trying not to. Her eyelids were pink, her eyes bloodshot. She was lying flat on her back with her bare feet crossed at the ankle, and her hands were resting on the middle of her stomach. And those ear buds were snuggly attached. She's always loved music— probably as much as you.

"I asked if she was hungry as I held out the paper plate that was bending under the weight of the greasy comfort food.

"She sat up, tucked her legs beneath her, and pocketed the iPod. 'Not really,' was all she said. I set the plate between us and offered her a bottle of water, watching her small fingers twist the cap back and forth as I struggled with my jacket until my arms were finally freed. I'm telling you, Ian, the suit was *bad*. But it did make a nice pillow. That horrible tie came off next and I tossed it to the floor before lying back.

"I told her it was a nice service, because I didn't know what else to say. All I knew was I wanted to talk to her. I wanted to take some of her sadness away.

"I felt that way about you too. Especially these past few months. I could see you weren't as happy as you were when we met.

"But I didn't know it was this bad.

"I...I didn't—I didn't know. I wish I had, but I just didn't see it.

"Maybe I didn't want to see it. Maybe my subconscious refused to accept it. I don't know.

"I don't know

"I don't know."

Fuck.

I run my fingers over my face roughly. "I need a minute. I'm sorry. I just need… I'll be back. I promise, I'm not leaving the hospital—I'm not leaving you. I'm going to take a walk and I'll be right back."

I skim my fingers over his pale cheeks. I've never seen someone look so ghostly white before. I hate it.

I *hate* it.

This isn't him. So still, so placid, so colorless.

I push the chair back with my legs as I stand and head straight for the door. I practically rip it off its hinges as I tear it open. I feel like I'm suffocating in this room.

I can't breathe.

I just need to get away.

This isn't my reality. It can't be. It's a long, twisted nightmare.

I'm going to wake up and Ian and I will be lying in bed. His palm will be flat against my chest, over my heart, like it is every morning. His wrists will be unmarked, soft and smooth how they always have been.

His eyes will flutter open, catching me looking at him while he sleeps. He'll smile and I'll lean in to capture it with my mouth. We'll both laugh easily and I'll tell him about the most horrific nightmare I have ever had. And he'll hold me, smoothing the hair away from my face as he assures me it would never happen because our love it too strong for such an awful thing to occur.

I'll make him promise me and he will. Sealing it with a kiss.

Because something like this doesn't happen to people like Ian and me. Not us. We're too happy and too in love.

Four

Ian

I never understood why it was called "falling in love."
It's not like there's a pit somewhere labeled "*Love,*" and
people are falling in, two at a time. It didn't make sense.

Not until now.

I wasn't looking for this. For *him.* I was just going
about my life and one day, I stumbled upon this man—tall,
blonde, beautiful, with eyes like an ocean and a voice that
sends shivers down my spine. I tripped over it—all of it, and
fell right onto my ass at his feet. Completely in love.

I want him. All of him. For now. For tomorrow.
Forever.

Sitting here on his couch, face to face, knees to knees,
while music filters through the small speaker of his iPod is
the singular most perfect moment of my life.

I want to kiss him. More than I want to eat or drink or

breathe.

So I do.

I lean forward, bringing my face close to his. His eyes are steady on me, watching me. The look on his face right now, tells me he knows what I'm getting ready to do and that he approves. He wants this too.

My hand is a little shaky as I reach for him. I think he notices, but doesn't comment. Instead, he wraps his fingers around mine securely and the trembling stops. My lips part in appreciation as he slides my hand around his neck, pulling me closer.

"I'd like to kiss you," he says. It's not a question, but he waits, giving me time to answer anyway even though we both know I was already headed there.

My only reply is to lean in closer, lick my lips, and press them to his. He holds perfectly still, letting my mouth form to his. It's not until I apply a small amount of pressure, asking to deepen the kiss that he finally reacts.

He takes over. His mouth opening, causing mine to open in the same motion. His tongue sweeps over mine like he's testing. Tasting.

I taste him back.

He's a little bit sweet, a little bit salty, and wholly flawless.

I love kissing him as much as I love loving him.

I never want this to end. I want to bask in the harmony of this instant for the rest of my days.

Five

Guy

On my walk, I pass room after room after room. All filled with people. Injured people. Sick people. Dying people.

They all have a story. A reason for being here. But all I care about is Ian and why he's here.

It's my fault.

I know it is.

We had a fight before I left for Chase and Annie's wedding. All because I wanted him there with me. I wanted my boyfriend at my side to watch one of my closest friends marry my stepsister. I wanted it so much, in fact, that I said some horrible things. Things I can't take back. Things that will haunt me always.

His first text came through during the wedding vows. Short and simple. *I'm sorry*.

The second on my way to the reception. *It won't*

always be this way.

The third during Chase and Annie's first dance as husband and wife. *Please forgive me.*

I stopped checking my phone after that because I was hurt and angry, and I felt that if he couldn't be with me in person, then whatever he had to say could wait. It didn't matter anyway, I had heard this all before, more times than I could count. And the wedding only amplified my pain because I knew I would never have the kind of life my friends have.

Hope is my best friend, my other half, my female counterpart. She knows all of my secrets—the good, the bad, and the ugly. The one and only person I tell everything to and trust with all that information. Everything except Ian.

I love her more than I've ever loved anyone. Except Ian.

I used to tell Hope how much I love her on a daily basis. But as we grew up and went our separate ways, I've told her less and less frequently. That's how life works, I guess. At some point, calling up your best friend just to say, "Hey, I love you," becomes a little weird the older you get. Especially after you fall in love.

I rested my arm on Hope's shoulder as we watched Chase and Annie cut their wedding cake—typical flowered towers, growing in size from top to bottom, with a small, ornate bride and groom perched on the highest layer. As the knife sliced through the cake, it might as well have been my heart.

On the other side of Hope, her husband, Mason, slipped his fingers in between hers. I stared at their hands for a long moment, and the same familiar pang registered in my chest.

Jealousy.

Not because Hope has Mason or Mason has Hope. I'm happy for them—always have been. I'd like to think I was responsible for bringing them together all those years ago.

The envy inside was because they're madly in love and disgustingly happy about it. In fact, everywhere I look there's a blissfully happy couple. The whole world knows just by looking at them. And I want to know that feeling.

How does it feel to share your happiness with all the people that mean the most to you?

I'm twenty-five. Ian's twenty-three. Much too old to have to hide. I know how difficult it can be, believe me. But I was so tired of faking my life.

When I first came out and Mom and Dad split up, I went crazy, searching for acceptance and love from someone—anyone—who might understand the turmoil poisoning my insides. For a long while, I kissed, sucked, and fucked any guy that showed interest. Because for those few minutes, I felt *good*.

It lessened the pain I held inside, but only added to the guilt I felt over my mom. Knowing I was not only responsible for the screaming matches between my parents, but also for their divorce, and then, ultimately, for my mom taking off and abandoning all three of her children, was often more than I could bear.

And in the back of my head, at all times, was the fact she didn't love me for who I was—who I am.

My sexuality and her religious beliefs clashed. Sides were taken, war ensued, and in the end, there was no victory. Only casualties. We all lost. A family torn apart. Over me.

Mom thought I was sick. Mentally. Spiritually. She thought she could pray the gay away. And when that didn't seem to work, she looked into shrinks, priests, camps, and counselors.

Seeing the toll it was taking on our family, Dad presented Mom with an ultimatum: Accept it or leave.

She was gone within the month. I've only seen her twice since then, and it was two too many times.

But I still love her. I still hold guilt.

I'm still gay.

And I didn't go through all of that just to hide now.

But somehow I'm still searching for the unconditional love all my friends have found. I thought I had that with Ian, but every time he pulled his hand away from mine when someone entered the room, it left a scar on my heart until I couldn't take the hurt anymore.

Cheers and laughter filled the air as Chase ran from Annie. He grabbed my arm, ducking behind me, hiding from his bride and the large clump of cake in her hand.

I realized what she was going to do half a second before she swung her arm. Though I tried to get out of the way, Chase was still holding onto me. Hope was on my other side. And I had nowhere to go.

Icing, fondant, and little pieces of red velvet cake splattered across my face and onto my shirt, jacket, and tie. I froze in stunned silence, peering down at myself. Chunks of frosting fell from my head and landed on my shoe with a wet plopping sound.

A bark of laughter sounded beside me and I glanced sideways at Hope. Her eyes were bright with amusement as she gripped my tie, tugging me down to her height, and licked the side of my face from my chin to my temple. Just a reminder as to why she's my best friend.

"Oh, it's good," she said, scooping more icing off with the tip of her finger and placing it in her mouth.

I licked my lips, noting that it was, in fact, delicious. Moist, soft, and sweet. And my thoughts instantly went back to Ian because he would have loved everything—from the cake to the attack to Hope eating it directly from my face.

After making sure Chase ended up messier than me—because come on, it was only fair—I went inside the house to start washing up.

That's when I finally pulled my phone back out.

I wish I had looked at it earlier. I wish I hadn't chosen to ignore the many texts Ian sent. Because I know now he was reaching out, begging me for help.

And I wasn't there.

Six

Ian

It's probably not normal to be happy about our first fight, but I can't hide the pleasant chill I get as Guy paces the length of the couch like a cheetah, sizing up his prey. It's sexy as hell.

The reason behind his anger is even sexier.

"It's one thing not to announce you have a boyfriend because you aren't announcing that you're gay. I hate it, but I can live with that. For now." He pauses, hands on hips, chest rising and falling with his quickened breaths as he pins me in place with his heated stare. "But having to sit by and keep my mouth shut while another man openly hits on you…that's too much."

"I think you're overreacting. He wasn't hitting on me. As far as he knows, I'm straight."

Guy's head lolls to the side in disbelief. "He was definitely hitting on you."

"He wasn't," I correct. "But does it even matter? I'm only interested in you. I only want you." I throw my hands out, gesturing toward him. "You. You. YOU. I could give a shit about anyone else."

He moves toward me slowly, dropping to his knees in front of the couch. His fingers dig into my sides as he pulls me to the edge, his anger gradually dissipating. "It matters because I didn't like it. It made me jealous and I'm not accustomed to feeling this way. Normally, I'd just tell the dude to back off my man, and I couldn't do that this time. I don't. Like. Feeling this way."

"I'm sorry," I murmur. The caveman jealously is cute—I've never had that before, but I hate that I make him feel anything other than happy. "Next time, I'll let him know I'm already taken."

One light brown brow lifts, that intensity once again shining in his eyes. "I want to *take* you right now."

Every muscle in my body clenches pleasantly with his declaration. "Then take me."

Without another word, Guy grabs my hand, pulling me off the couch, and tows me into his bedroom. His scent is on everything, filling the room. I inhale deeply, taking it in and letting his smell oxygenize my cells as they flow through my blood.

He undresses me, pulling me shirt over my head before unbuttoning my jeans. When I'm in nothing but my boxers, I return the favor, stripping him of the layers separating us.

He kisses me. Soft, slow. My fingers dig into his cheeks as I stifle a moan. Every kiss always feels better than the last. His teeth sink into my tongue hard enough to make me wince before a new rush of desire washes over me. One where my movements become rough, rushed, and clumsy.

I slide my fingers behind his neck and fist them into his hair. I give it a little tug enjoying the way his breath catches. His hand presses into my back, pulling me tight against his body. I can feel every rigid muscle in his abdomen. Skin to skin. And lower, I feel the solid evidence of his need.

I like sex. I have from the very first time I tried it. I'm also versatile—I like to give pleasure as much as I like to receive it. But this is our first time together. So I let him lead.

Guy lowers himself to the ground, his chest grazing my front all the way down. I'm throbbing. I'm so ready for this. Have been since the day we met.

His fingers curl into the waistband of my boxers and he slides them down, the movement measured, deliberately slow.

My erection springs free, making Guy smile up at me.

"I love that I do this to you."

I love it too, but I don't tell him this because if I say anything right now with the word love in it, it won't be about my hard cock. It will be about him. How much I've fallen in love with him. And we're not there yet. Not until I can bring him home to meet my family. Not until I can hold his hand at the store. Not until I can tell a random stranger hitting on me that I have a boyfriend.

Guy takes me into his hand as he runs his hot tongue over my engorged length from the tip to the hilt and back again. I hiss though my teeth, fisting my fingers into his hair. He keeps up a tortured pace, bringing me closer and closer to the edge.

He pulls back, running his finger under his lip. "I want to be inside you. I want to make you feel good," he husks. "Get on the bed."

I do what he says, hopping onto his bed and stretching out on my back. I watch him wiggle out of his boxer-briefs, admiring the beauty of his naked form. Solid muscles, firm and all man. Sexy beyond belief.

The mattress dips under his weight as he crawls over me. His arms are positioned on either side of my head, holding his weight above me, but I want to feel him on top of me. I nudge his inner elbow, causing him to drop. He laughs and I wrap my arms around him as I close my mouth over his.

His laughter fades quickly, replaced with a feverish desire as he kisses me back.

Unable to wait, I reach between us and stroke him. He's silky smooth and I love the way he feels in my hand. Like he was made for me.

Guy reaches over, tugging a condom from the bedside drawer. I take it from him, opening it with my teeth, and roll it on, sheathing him. It's my way of letting him know I'm ready.

His forehead touches mine for a moment, his breath dancing across my skin. And then he's pushing inside as slowly as he took me into his mouth. He stretches my legs up, using one to rest his chest on as he grips my pulsing length. His hand matches the rhythm of his thrusts and I'm gone. So gone. Lost in a cloudy haze of euphoria.

It's never felt this good before. But I've never done this with someone I love before, either.

It's amazing. As perfect as he is.

Seven

Guy

I find myself back at the door to Ian's room. I have no idea how long I've been gone. Time no longer has meaning.

I push it open hesitantly, almost afraid of what I'll find on the other side. But he's exactly as I left him, unmoving, silent.

My feet take me across the room on their own accord. They don't stop until I'm standing in front of the window. I peer outside, taking in the depressing view of the emergency room parking lot. Every space is filled. Must be a busy night for tragedy.

Picking up where I stopped earlier, as if I never left the room, I lower myself into the chair and start talking.

"I know I've told you this before, but it's a good story. My first hetero kiss. And kind of my only, because even though I had a few, they were all with Hope. But the first, that's the most important.

"I couldn't sleep after Uncle Donnie's funeral. My mind was busy with too many thoughts. Like how I'd never...I'd never see my uncle again. How I was just getting to really know him before he died much too young. How that one motorcycle ride we took would be the only I'd ever have with him.

"My heart hurt and I didn't want to feel that way."

I look at Ian, my eyes trailing over his face. His dark lashes, thick and long, resting on his cheeks. His nose, a tiny bit crooked but incredibly adorable. And his lips, soft and slightly blue.

"Is that how you felt all the time? Like your heart hurt? You should have told me. I could have helped you."

I close my eyes—I can't stomach to look at him this way—and continue with my story.

"I knew Hope was just a floor below me. I knew she was probably having trouble sleeping too. If I was that tore up over my step-uncle, I couldn't imagine how much she was hurting over her *mom*.

"I tried to think about losing my mom or dad and had to quickly push it away. Despite everything my mom's done to me, all the hurtful things she's said, and how angry I was with her, the thought of her no longer living made me sick to my stomach.

"I decided I'd just go check. If Hope was asleep, I'd go back to bed and count sheep or something. But if she was awake, it'd be proof, like a sign that she needed someone. And since I needed someone right then too, I figured we could be each other's someone.

"I maneuvered around the creaky step—the one I've told you about, the one that got me caught sneaking out on more than one occasion. I always hated those stairs.

"Hope sat up immediately and I plopped down beside her like it was the most normal thing in the world, and I asked her, 'If you could go anywhere right now, where would you go?'

"She blew out a breath and you know what she said? 'I'd go back in time five days ago and stop my mom and Donnie from leaving.' Just like that.

"Her answer caught me off guard, but I covered my surprise and asked her another random question. And then another and another, and before I knew it, it was four in the morning.

"We were both yawning, so I decided to ask one last question before calling it a night: 'Who was your first kiss?'

"She bit her lip, looked down at her folded hands in her lap, and shrugged. She told me she had never been kissed. And even in the darkness, I knew she was embarrassed.

"I don't know what possessed me to do it. I had never wanted to kiss a girl—not once in my life before that night and never again since—but I leaned over her and brushed the hair off of her shoulders.

"Maybe it was because I wanted to do something for her. Maybe it was because I felt comfortably close with her right then.

"Hell, maybe it was just because I had never kissed a girl before... But I placed my hands on each side of her face and tilted her head so I could reach her better. And then I kissed her. She didn't react at first, so I slipped my tongue between her lips until it touched hers.

"She kissed me back then. I was so torn because even though I wasn't attracted to her, I liked kissing her. But it's not so much the actual kiss that I liked. I think I liked that I was her first. And she was mine. I liked that I was able to find something on that horrible day to make her forget, even if only for a moment. To make us both forget.

"She was my first girl kiss. On the fourth worst day of my life, she was my silver lining.

"I could have been that for you. I could have been your silver lining. If you had just asked."

I squeeze my eyes, my teeth gnashing together. The longer I sit in this hospital, the more scared I become. The more scared I become, the angrier I get.

"I know we fought," I husk. "I know I pushed too hard sometimes. I can be an asshole, I know that. But what did I do that was so bad? Want you? Love you?

"What did I do that justified this?" I toss my hand out toward the bed, though he can't see the gesture.

"What did I do that made you rather die than be with me?"

The tears I've been fighting finally spill over, running down my cheeks in heated streaks. My chest feels tight, my airway constricted.

"I need to know.

"What did I do?

"What?

"WHAT DID I DO?

"*What did I do?*"

An angry calm settles over me. There's a humming in my ears, in my head. I feel my body sway in the chair.

"You're so selfish, Ian. How could you do this to me? How could you try to leave me like this? Didn't you care how I would feel? Didn't you care about what losing you would do to me? Did you think about me at all?

"No. Only *your* pain mattered. Only you.

"Always you."

I'm gasping for breath now, staring hard into his face that doesn't look like his face.

"I'm sorry," I sob. "I'm so sorry."

"I'm sorry."

"I'm sorry."

"I'm sorry."

Eight

Ian

"Sometimes you just need to let it be," I hiss. "Just once, just let someone else be right. Or be wrong, but shut the hell up about it."

I'm irrationally angry, I know it, but I can't stop the poison that keeps seeping from my lips.

"Maybe if you'd nag less, I'd be more inclined to go places with you."

BAM.

It just keeps coming and coming, no end in sight.

"You are the neediest little boy I've ever met."

POW.

"I can't even stand to look at you when you're like this."

CRUSH.

"Just go without me because I don't want to be

anywhere near you."

CRASH.

"GO. Get the fuck out. You'd rather be with them anyway. So. Just. Go."

SMASH.

He just stands there, head cast down, waiting for me to finish. I can't stand it. It makes me want to scream more. Hurt him more.

The last thing I ever want to do is hurt him.

What the fuck is wrong with me?

I can't make it stop. I don't know how.

I pick up the closest thing to me, a half-full bottle of water, and launch it across the room. It smacks the wall hard and falls to the ground. It's not enough. Not nearly enough.

I grab the frame sitting on the end table—a photo of Hope and Guy—and fling it to the ground. The sound of the glass splintering breaks through my angered haze.

I didn't mean to do that. I didn't mean to break it.

Guy picks it up, turning it over in his hands. There's a crack running from one corner to the other. He blinks slowly. "I just won't go. We can order in and rent a movie." He sets the frame back on the table and disappears into the bedroom.

As soon as the door shuts, something takes hold of me again.

I stalk toward the room, throwing the door open. It hits the wall, bouncing back toward me. I kick it this time and the knob smashes into the drywall, holding the door in place. Guy stands up from the bed, watching me. Unsure. Uneasy.

I've never hit him, but he's watching me like that's exactly what I'm going to do. It kills me and infuriates me at the same time.

Without a word, I take hold of his arm, pushing his back into the wall. He doesn't question me as I push his pants down to his knees, exposing him. He doesn't ask me to stop as I stretch one of his arms out, palm flat to the wall, followed by the other.

Then I drop to my knees and grasp him in my hand.

I want to make him pay for making feel this way.

I want to tell him I'm sorry for feeling this way— acting this way.

I take him into my mouth and do both.

There's something wrong with me. I don't understand how he can care about me. Why he stays with me. Why he would ever want to be with a person as useless as I am.

I have to show him I'm worth something.

Moisture pools in my eyes so I close them. I don't want him to see. He'll think I'm crying because of something he did. Something he said. But it's never him. It's me. Only me.

He'd be better off without me. So much better if I didn't exist. I'm only holding him back.

So many enemies inside my head and they're all me.

Nine

Guy

"You're probably wondering why I look like this," I say quietly.

I'm still in my suit, covered in wedding cake and icing. And now Ian's blood. My pants are still damp from the bath water when I pulled his lifeless body from the tub.

"I came straight from the reception as soon as I saw your texts."

I'm sorry.

It won't always be this way.

Please forgive me.

Please answer me.

I need you.

I can't live without you.

I won't live without you.

Please come home.

Never mind. It's too late.

I love you.

"I stared at the texts, reading and rereading them. You didn't say it, you didn't tell me what you did, but I...I just felt it.

"It was the last one—the *I love you.*

"You've never said it before and I knew...it felt like a goodbye.

"I should have called 911. I shouldn't have wasted the time to drive home.

"I should have been with you."

The door opens and I step back quickly, wiping my eyes with the backs of my hands. Ian's mom steps into the room. I'm shocked, but try to hide it. His parents live nine hours away. I wasn't expecting them this soon. I look at the clock for the first time since I got Ian's texts.

Has it been that long?

Mrs. Miccoli's gaze moves almost unseeingly over

me, settling on her son. She takes in his palled skin, the bandages circling his wrists, the tubes running from his arm and his nose. And she breaks.

A noise—guttural and agonized—erupts from her throat. She moves toward the bed, her eyes wide and brimming with tears.

"Why?" she asks.

"Why? Why? Why?"

I don't think she's asking me. I don't even think she's asking Ian. Maybe God. Maybe the fates. Maybe the universe.

Maybe no one at all.

It doesn't matter. I don't think there's an answer. Not one we can understand, anyway.

I shouldn't be here. Ian wouldn't like it—me alone with his mom, my emotions so obvious. After taking one last look at his face, I pivot on my heel and leave as quickly as I possibly can.

In the hall I move faster, trying to escape this prison.

When I burst through the doors, there's no relief. Everything remains fucked up. Only now, it's fucked up under a starry sky.

Going against Ian's wishes, I take my phone from my pocket and dial Hope's number. And when she answers, her voice full of sleep and confused concern, I tell her everything—the truth about Ian and me. From our first date all the way up until I kicked the bathroom door in and found him floating in a pool of his own blood.

Ten

Ian

I want to tell him I love him every day. That I've never loved anyone more. But it continues to sit on my tongue, unsaid.

But I feel it. I feel it in every inch of my body. My heart. My soul. Always.

Today, another feeling is stronger. The beastly demon I fight against every minute of every day. I won't be getting out of bed, and I know it's going to piss Guy off. At first, I hid it well. After a couple of months, it became harder to hide. He was understanding for those first few months. But now, it's grown old. His patience has run out.

I'm not sick with a virus. I haven't caught a bug. But I am physically ill. The best way I can describe it is like poison, swimming through my veins, draining everything from me.

My head is foggy—that's always the hardest to ignore. Like my mind is thick with the poison, swirling, swirling, swirling. My body is heavy, my blood weighed down, syrupy and coagulated. It takes all of my energy just to roll over. I can't imagine trying to get up right now.

Sleep.

All I want to do is sleep.

My stomach hurts. I feel as if I might vomit. It might just be the fog, making me dizzy and lightheaded. It messes with my equilibrium. Or it could be the anxiety building because I know this is going to cause another argument with Guy.

And that's just the physical.

All the negative thoughts racing through my mind make me want to scream. To rip my ears off, though I know that's not where I hear the thoughts.

It's not voices.

It just one voice.

My own.

Telling me I'm not good enough. Telling me I never will be. Insisting that my parents' lives would be so much easier without me. That Guy would be happier. That I could end so much suffering.

When I was younger, thirteen-fourteen, I would sneak into my dad's office. I'd take the key he kept hidden in his top, right desk drawer, and I would open the little lockbox he didn't know I knew about.

I'd sit in his chair, spinning, spinning in circles, lockbox in lap. Then I'd take the gun out of the velvety case, and I'd hold it to my head.

I never checked to see if it was loaded. I never checked to see if the safety was on. Hell, I don't even know if it *had* a safety. I never cocked it. And I never pulled the trigger. But I would close my eyes, spinning around and around, gripping that gun like a life vest.

Like it was my savior.

I haven't done that since the day I left for college. Haven't even thought about it until recently.

I wish I could tell Guy about my dad's gun. I don't think I ever will, though. He'd think I was insane. He'd be worried. Maybe even mad. I've pissed him off enough lately.

So instead, I'll just stay in bed.

Eleven

Guy

Unable to sleep in the home I share with Ian—in the bed we share as a couple, I drain the tub and begin cleanup on the bathroom. No matter how much bleach I use, I can't un-see the blood. It's a blaring red sign of Ian's pain. Smeared on the floor, stained in the grout of the shower walls, soaked into the bath rug.

The fingertips of my rubber gloves are caked in my boyfriend's agony.

I need it gone. I need it off of me.

Now.

NOW.

Scrubbing harder, quicker, I keep going. More bleach. More cleanser. I dump the bucket of water and get new. Another sponge. Another scrub brush. Faster. Faster. Faster.

And when I can no longer see it, I strip off my soiled suit and shove every piece into the trash before cleansing myself in the same place Ian tried to end his life.

~*~

I step out of the shower, wrap a towel around my waist, and wipe the condensation from the mirror.

I don't recognize the stranger reflected there. Dark circles around his normally light eyes, red-rimmed and bloodshot. But it's the look on his face that won't let me look away. This man looks broken. Like he's beaten down and giving up. That's not who I am. I'm the happy one. The easy-going, playful one. The one who's always smiling. Joking. Laughing.

My eyes close and I know the man's in the mirror do too. I turn away, dressing quickly. I need to get back to the hospital. I know I can't stay in his room, but I need to be close by for when he wakes up.

I leave a message on my boss's voicemail, letting him know I won't be in for a few days. I don't give him details, but he knows me. He knows I wouldn't take time off without a good reason.

After four years in college, you'd think I'd be basking in my dream job—which I would be if I knew what that was. For now I'm stuck with a liberal arts degree and a full-time bartending gig at a club I would never go into if I wasn't getting paid to do so.

But I have to pay the bills somehow and I'd rather do what I do than ever have to ask for a handout.

Ian works from home, writing for a small news website. I know he's not working in his ideal career, either, but it's convenient for him. He can do it all from home and never have to leave the apartment, which he prefers.

I drop onto the couch, resting my feet on the arm. I just need a minute. Just sixty seconds where I can pretend everything is normal. I get about twenty before there's a very distinctive knock on the door.

I push myself off the couch and hurry to answer it.

"Open up, I need to pee," Chase yells from the hallway.

I huff out a light laugh as I open the door. He pushes past me, booking ass toward the bathroom. "I got up and came straight here before I went," he utters. "And Park had to stop for coffee on the way." He keeps talking, but his voice is muffled behind the confines of the door. I can only make out the words "creamer" and "ass" and decide I probably don't want to know what he's saying anyway.

Park, one of my closest friends for as long as I can remember, shakes his head as he steps inside. "My daughter isn't even that bad. I swear he has a bladder the size of a peanut."

"Only if his bladder is the same size as his balls," I reply automatically.

He chuckles, running a hand through his dark hair before setting his Styrofoam cup on the table. He opens his mouth to reply, but is cut off by Chase as he pops his head out of the door.

"That's offensive," he calls.

"To *peanuts*," Park retorts under his breath.

"I heard that," Chase yells.

"I don't give a shit," Park sings.

I sigh. This feels good. This feels *normal*. My friends giving each other shit over absolutely nothing. I needed this.

Park settles onto the couch, his head falling back against the cushion just as Chase joins us. We all sit there in silence for several seconds. And then Chase sits forward, resting his elbows on his knees and says, "Peanuts are good for you."

"Are you defending your sack size?" Park asks, his head rolling to look at Chase. "Because that's just sad."

"No, I'm saying you can eat my nuts, jackass."

I smirk at Park and give a little shrug. "High in protein."

He lifts a brow, letting his eyes fall closed. "But not very filling."

"You sound so gay right now," I laugh.

"You must be rubbing off on me," he quips, his lips lifting into something that could be considered a smile. "Don't tell my wife. She might take that the wrong way."

"Your wife adores me," I remind him. "Oh, and speaking of wives..." I glance at Chase. "How's your bride?"

He grins. "At rubbing me off? She's good. Very, very, *good.*"

"No," I deadpan. "Just...no, no, no."

He chuckles, unabashed. "She's in her happy place—making sure all the last minute details are set for the honeymoon."

"When do you leave?"

"This afternoon. Hawaii, baby."

"Lucky bastard," Park mutters.

"Today?" I verify. "And she let you out? How'd you pull that off?"

Chase's smile fades. He rubs his palms over his knees and presses his lips together. "Hope told us about your roommate. Thought you might need some company."

I nod tightly. I have the best fucking friends in the world. They don't even know how much Ian means to me—he's so much more than my roommate—and yet they took time out of their lives to check on me.

I nod again, unable to find words.

"They have macadamia nuts in Hawaii," Park says.

~*~

After Park and Chase leave, I grab my keys, ready to head out when someone knocks at my door. Again.

My eyes flick to the clock, noting the time. My elderly next-door neighbor fills her days watching cooking shows. Once or twice a week, Val will have a bake fest, and then she brings Ian and me all sorts of goodies. Ian loves her oatmeal raisin cookies. I hope she made some so I can take them up to the hospital for him.

I pull the door open, expecting my small seventy-year-old neighbor, but instead am met with my small twenty-five-year-old best friend.

She doesn't say anything—she doesn't need to. I can read everything she's thinking from the expression on her face. Her arms open, inviting me in for a hug. I can't remember the last time we've had to reverse roles this way, her comforting me. But I accept immediately.

I wrap my arms around her tiny frame, burying my face into her hair. The wall I've built up since leaving the hospital splinters, leaving cracks and holes in the structure. I don't know what it is about a hug, but there is no better damage to a person's armor.

I cry. I cry hard. I cry long.

Hope backs me out of the doorway and into the apartment, kicking the door closed without ever letting go of me. Her hands rub soothing circles into my back as I soak her shirt with my pain.

Finally, when I have no more tears to cry, I pull away, rubbing the moisture from my face.

"Why didn't you tell me?" she asks. There's no judgment in her voice. Just a curiosity, and maybe a little hurt.

I shake my head stiffly. "He didn't want me to tell anyone."

"Eleven months, though, Guy—" She closes her mouth abruptly, cutting herself off. "It doesn't matter. It's the least important thing right now. How is he? What did the doctors say?"

"I haven't been back up there since his mom got there, but last I heard he was stable and doing well. I was actually on my way out when you got here."

"I'll go with you," she says quietly, tucking a lock of dark hair behind her ear. "I don't want you to be alone. Oh, by the way, did Tweedle Dee and Tweedle Dum come by?"

"Yeah. They were a good distraction."

She smiles. "Good."

"I thought you and Mason were going back to Chicago today?"

"We were, but now we're not. You've always been there for me when I needed you. It's long overdue that I repay the favor." She pokes me in the stomach with her index finger. "Besides," she adds, "I want to hear more about your relationship with Ian. It's strange to think of him as your boyfriend when I've never known him to be anything more than your friend and roommate. I'm usually so much better at picking up on these things."

Twelve

Ian

Guy and I are trying our hands at cooking. "Trying" being the key word. We're both terrible cooks. Absolutely horrible. We burnt the lasagna. I caught the cheeseburgers on fire. And Guy charred the grilled cheese he decided to make after we doused the burger flames. The smoke detectors are screaming in anguish. It would be sad if it weren't so funny.

"What do you want on the pizza?" Guy yells over his shoulder as he waves a towel in the air, trying to waft the smoke away from the fire alarm.

"Everything," I say. "I'm starving."

He chuckles, his eyes full of mirth. "Maybe we should take cooking classes."

"Maybe?" I scoff. "I think it's a must."

"It's probably a safety issue at this point," he adds, smirking at me. "I bet this is why Val bakes for us. She undoubtedly thinks we'd starve without her cookies."

"What's scary is that we probably would."

He shakes his head, grinning. "Nah, as long as I can still hit the speed dial on my phone for takeout, we'll be all right." He winks as he pulls our ruined lasagna off of the counter, taking it to the sink.

I shake my head sadly. "It's a shame. It smelled good before it got charred. My mom makes awesome pasta dishes. Next time I go home, I'll ask her to make me one to bring home so you can try it."

He busies himself, scraping all of our failed attempts at dinner into the food disposal, his gaze intently set on his task. "Do you think I'll ever get to meet her? Your mom? As your friend or your roommate even?"

He has no idea how much I want to introduce them.

I wrap my arms around him from behind, pressing a kiss into his neck. He smells so good. Like standing on your porch on a summer's night and inhaling the fresh, earthy scent of nature. I breathe deeply, holding him in my lungs.

"You will. I promise."

"What's she like?" he murmurs. "Tell me about her."

"Mom is smart. She loves to read. And I inherited my writing gene from her. She's a brilliant cook, though Val puts Mom's oatmeal cookies to shame."

Guy turns in my arms, his hands gripping my sides. "Oh, I am so telling her you said that. It will go like this: Hi Mrs. Miccoli. It's nice to meet the woman whose vagina squeezed Ian out. Thanks for not using any birth control. Oh, by the way, Ian said another woman's cookies are better than yours. Can you make me a lasagna?"

I nod thoughtfully. "You should ask for the lasagna first. That way she'll be thinking about whether or not she has all the ingredients. It might distract from the rest of it."

He grins widely. "Duly noted. But seriously, she sounds great."

"She is," I agree.

"She would have to be—she made you." He touches his lips to mine. This is my favorite kind of kiss. The kind where nothing is expected. When we just hold onto each other, sharing each other's breath.

These moments make me feel cherished. Loved. Complete.

If I could, I'd save them, every single one of them. I'd freeze them, and shrink-wrap them, and store them away for the times I lose myself.

If only it were possible. I would never have another bad day again.

"I love you," Guy whispers. "I know you have a hard time hearing it and an even harder time saying it, but I wanted you to know that's how I feel."

I don't know how to reply, but he doesn't give me the opportunity anyway. His mouth covers mine, kissing me deeply. His hands move upward, skimming my shirt up and over my head.

I'm no longer hungry. At least not for food.

Thirteen

Guy

When Hope and I get to Ian's room, his parents go to grab some much-needed coffee.

I pull the chair up to his bed, just as I did last night. Hope settles in the corner, pretending like she isn't watching me.

Ian's color is better today. And his hand is warmer, I notice, as I curl my fingers with his. I brush the hair away from his face because I need to see him.

"I've been thinking about Christmas," I say to him, unconcerned Hope's in the room. "I don't know why, but I just keep replaying the whole month of December in my head.

"It was a good month. You were so happy. We spent the first weekend decorating. Garland and lights around the windows. A wreath made of bells on the door—every time we opened or closed it, the bells would ring. I miss that sound.

"You bought those candles, you know, the ones that were striped like candy canes. And you were so mad when they didn't smell. So I brought you home a pack of candy canes the next day after work. It was just a dollar pack of candy, but you acted like it was the best gift in the world." I huff out a breathy laugh. "You smelled like peppermint for days because you were constantly eating them.

"Then the following weekend, you pulled out a ream of white computer paper and scissors, and we made snowflakes while we watched Christmas cartoons and drank hot chocolate.

"I felt like a little kid, but in all the best ways.

"And when the movie was over, we hung the paper snowflakes from the ceiling with fishing line. The end result was almost magical.

"We got our tree later that week. A real one because you love the smell. We bundled up and went to four different places before we found the perfect tree. And it was perfect, wasn't it?" I laugh again, this time with tears in my eyes.

"We tried to string popcorn, but I kept crumbling mine and you kept nicking yourself with the needle. We ended up tearing the garland off the windows and using it instead. And then we ate the popcorn."

I lose it here. Because it was my favorite Christmas. It was my favorite Christmas because he made it perfect. And now he's not here to share the memory.

What if he isn't here to make more memories with?

What if the memories I have are all I'll ever get?

The tears drop unendingly and I don't try to stop them. And I don't bother to wipe them away. I just let them come.

It isn't fair.

The good times far outweigh the bad. He can't give up.

He can't.

"On New Year's Eve, we made resolutions. You made mine for me and I made yours for you. We wrote them down and exchanged them at midnight. I said you needed to get out more and no more moping in bed. I remember the look on your face when you read it. You weren't mad or sad. You were disappointed. In me.

"And then I read your resolutions for me and I understood why.

"*You're perfect the way you are.* That's what you wrote."

I put my hand over my mouth, trying to quiet the sound of my sobs.

"You're perfect the way you are. I should have said that to you, Ian. I should have told you that every day.

"You're perfect. You're perfect to me. You're perfect for me.

"I love you. I love you so much. Please wake up so I can tell you.

"I need you to know."

Hope's arms circle around my waist, startling me. I grip the shoulder of her shirt, wrenching her tightly to me, and I cling to her.

"I should have told him," I whisper. "I should have told him."

Her body trembles violently and I realize she's crying too. For me. For Ian.

"It'll be okay," she utters.

I want to believe her. I really do. But I don't see how anything will ever be okay again. I've never felt so desolate. Never in my life.

"I need him," I husk. "He makes me so happy. I love him. *I need him.*" I feel her head bob against my chest in a nod, but she doesn't reply. There's not much that can be said.

And then I feel pressure on my hand—the one holding Ian's. My eyes dart first to our hands, observing the way his purposely curves around mine, and then to his face. I'm met with his soft blue eyes and I'm speechless. So grateful and relieved and scared and happy all at once.

"Guy?" he rasps. "Why are you crying?"

Fourteen

Ian

Guy doesn't need to tell me. I see the bandage on my wrist and it all comes back in slow chunks.

The pain.

The wedding.

The pain.

The argument.

The Pain.

The texts.

The PAIN.

The razor.

THE PAIN.

The blood.

It figures I can't even do that right.

"Get a nurse," he finally says to Hope. She moves around to the opposite side of the bed, pushing the call button. Guy grips my hand tighter, his features morphing back and forth between smiling and crying.

"I was so scared I'd never hear your voice again."

His voice is full of misery. Because of me. Because of what I did.

"I'm sorry," I croak. And I am. I never meant to hurt him. That was never my intent. There was just too much hurt. *Unbearable* hurt.

"I'm sorry," I repeat. I'm at a loss for words. Tired. Guilty. Sad. Ashamed.

"It's okay," he soothes. "It's okay."

"I'm sorry."

The nurse comes in and everything gets fuzzy and confusing. Guy and Hope are shuffled out. The nurse asks me questions and I think I answer them.

She tells me someone will be in to evaluate me.

She tells me I'm under a twenty-four hour watch.

She tells me I'm lucky.

She tells me everyone was worried about me.

She tells me my parents will be in soon.

She tells me I can't go home yet.

I'm humiliated.

Everyone knows what I did. And everyone will know for the rest of my life because I now where the evidence on my wrists, like emblems of my weakness.

I don't know why I did it. It seems like a dream now. Like it wasn't me.

I feel very alone.

Fifteen

Guy

My hands are on my head, my fingers locked into my hair. I pace, back and forth, back and forth, back and forth, in front of Ian's door.

He's awake.

The worry is still there, clinging to my shoulders, but no matter what happens from here on out, today is a good day.

He's awake.

And then I say it aloud to make it real, make it concrete.

"He's awake." I laugh with relief. With happiness. With more relief.

I look at Hope, leaning against the wall, watching me. She smiles. "He's awake," she echoes.

"I want to be in there with him."

She presses her lips together, forming a thin line. "He's going to need an evaluation. He won't be allowed visitors until they assess him."

"How long?" I utter. I come to a halt, my body rigid in anticipation of her answer. I can tell from her expression she doesn't want to tell me. I close my eyes and repeat the question. "How long?"

"It depends on the hospital's policy and what the doctor decides. Typically, anywhere between twenty-four hours to a week. They have a mental health ward here in the hospital, so that might make a difference. But once that's over, they'll probably set him up with outpatient care and let him go home."

This is what Hope has spent years in school for. Learning how to help people like Ian. People like herself. People with emotional and mental problems.

"When he comes home, what do I do? How do I take care of him? What if he tries to do it again?"

She takes my hand, tugging gently. "Let's go somewhere and talk. We shouldn't be doing this in front of his door."

I nod and follow her to the small waiting room. She takes a seat, gesturing for me to sit with her, but I have too much energy to sit. I shake my head, choosing to stand instead.

"I think first, you need to find out where Ian's going to go when he leaves."

"What do you mean? He'll go home. With me."

She bites down on her lip, her eyes flicking over my face as if she's trying to decide how to word her next sentence. "Shit dusted in sugar is still shit," I say. "Just say what's on your mind."

"He may want to go home with his parents. Sometimes after a suicide attempt, the person needs a change of environment."

He hasn't lived with his parents in over five years. I can't see him wanting to do it now. But maybe he needs to get away from me.

Now I sit.

"Sometimes they need consistency," Hope continues. "He very well may want to go home with you, but I want you to be prepared for either outcome. And there's also the chance that they might decide Ian needs more treatment than can be provided by outpatient care. They might decide to commit him. It's unlikely, but possible."

I drop my head into my hands. This is too much. I never thought this far ahead. I just wanted him to wake up so I could take him home. So I could be better with him. Take care of him.

"It's my fault," I husk. "We had a fight. He didn't want to come to Chase and Annie's wedding. And I...I told him I hated living a lie and that I wasn't going to do it anymore." I pinch my eyes closed, unable to look at her. "I told him he better hope I didn't find a better man at the wedding because I would replace him."

The guilt takes hold of my chest, squeezing and twisting.

"I didn't mean it. I was just mad. And hurt. And I wanted him with me. I shouldn't have said it."

"Guy," Hope says, her voice firm, angered. I don't want to see the look on her face. I keep my head down and my eyes closed. I deserve whatever she's about to say.

"This isn't your fault."

My breath hitches.

"Generally speaking, people who attempt to kill themselves are sick. I can't say for sure, but Ian probably has a chemical imbalance in his brain, like a sickness. And I'm guessing he's been sick for a very long time. He hid it well. But think about the toll that probably took on his already unstable mind. And on top of dealing with his illness by himself and keeping it from everyone, he was also hiding the fact that he's gay. That's a lot of stress for one person."

"That's why I know it's my fault. I pushed him when he already had so much to deal with."

Hope grips my chin, lifting it until I'm looking at her. She shakes her head stiffly. "No. Imagine you're holding a fifty-pound weight in one had—that represents mental illness. And in the other, you're holding another fifty-pound weight—that represents all of the secrets. You're a strong man, but the longer you hold those weights up, the heavier they're going to feel until they finally give out.

"He could have gone to the wedding with you. Or you could have stayed home. Ian probably would have still tried to hurt himself. It just would have come at a different time.

"What you need to understand is that everyone has arguments. Everyone says things they don't mean to their significant other. But then most couples either split up or make up. Most people don't try to kill themselves. Ian did this because he has an illness. Not because you argued. He's. Sick. If he had cancer, would you think he developed it because you were mad?"

I shake my head. I understand what she's saying—it's just hard to believe.

"You can't blame yourself. That's one of the most important things to remember because I can guarantee Ian doesn't blame you. And if he sees you beating yourself up, that's going to make him and you both feel horrible."

"Okay," I whisper. That I can understand. I don't want to make him feel worse in any way. I'll fake it if I have to.

"Okay?"

I nod. "Okay."

She sighs. "It'll take some time. I know it's not easy to change an impression once you've thought it and believed it. It's probably a good idea for you to talk to a counselor. This has affected you too."

I just nod again, not wanting to get into this. Ian is the one who matters most right now. Once he's taken care of, then I'll worry about me.

"What about when he comes home." I pause, meeting her gaze. "I heard you and am prepared that he might not come home, but talk to me as if he is. What should I anticipate?"

Hope blows out a breath, lifting her hair away from her face. "Don't bombard him, but don't leave him alone, either. Most failed suicide attempts don't try a second time. Some do, though, so you need to make sure you don't have anything in your apartment that will make another attempt easy. If he wants to do it that bad, he'll find a way no matter what, but you want to make it as hard for him as you can."

Talking to Hope, of all people, is almost surreal. She suffered years of self-harm, so when she tells me Ian will find a way if he truly wants to, I believe her.

"Get rid of the sharp objects—razors, knives, things like that. Make sure there aren't any medications other than the ones the doctors prescribed. Even over the counter medications like Tylenol. Often they can be worse than prescribed medicine. And you stay in charge of those. Don't let him. Not yet.

"He's probably going to have a lot of self-guilt, anger, embarrassment. Don't push him to talk about it—that's what the doctors are for. He might never want to talk to you about this, but listen if he decides he does.

"Other than that, make sure he's eating healthy. Vitamins are a good idea. Encourage him to get exercise because it gives you natural endorphins and endorphins make you feel good. You guys could work out together. And most of all, just be there for him, but don't neglect yourself. You're no good to him if you're in a bad place."

"That's a lot to remember," I say. "My brain is on overload. I'm kind of afraid I'll forget something. I'm also terrified I'll fuck something up."

"I'll send you info and links to help you remember. You'll be fine. I promise. Just do what you're best at."

"What's that?"

"Love him."

Sixteen

Ian

They said twenty-four hours, but it's been forty-two since I last saw Guy. In that time, I've been moved to the mental ward. Just the thought makes me feel worthless.

I've spoken to four nurses and three different doctors. I've answered more questions in the past two days than I have in most of my life. But I've answered them openly and honestly, even when they repeated the same questions five different ways.

Because I want to get better.

Because I want to live.

Because I want a good life.

Because I want to live that good life with Guy.

The doctors placed me on three separate medications. I wonder if each doctor prescribed me something or if they all got together and discussed it. Either way, I now have an array of pills to swallow every day.

I don't know if they're helping. The doctors said it will take time for my body to adjust and see a difference. So far they just make me kind of sleepy.

I hope they work. I hope they can make me better.

The nurse—Gina, a woman old enough to be my grandmother—said I could see my parents today. No friends yet, but if my visit goes well today, I might be allowed more visitors tomorrow. And it's possible I'll be allowed to go home at the end of the week.

I'm not holding my breath. I'm scared to see my parents. I'm afraid they'll ask me why I did this to myself. I'm afraid I won't be able to answer and I'll hurt them even more.

I don't want to hurt anyone.

My wrists are healing well, Gina tells me. I just take her word for it. I've refused to look at the wounds when she changes my bandages. But when my arms are wrapped, they're all I can stare at.

I've been thinking, because that's all there really is to do here, and I've come to the conclusion that having the scars will be good. Little reminders so I never try this again. I hope I never actually need a reminder, but they'll be there just in case.

The door opens and my mom peers around the corner. Her dark hair—the same color as mine—is smoothed into a ponytail perfectly, but she has dark rings around her puffy eyes.

She's lost sleep.

She's been crying.

It doesn't take a genius to figure out why.

I'm sorry.

I'm so sorry.

"Hi, honey," she says softly. "How are you feeling?"

How am I feeling?

Disgusting.

Worthless.

Guilty.

Stupid.

Pathetic.

"Okay. How are you?"

She smiles weakly. "I'm good."

My dad follows her in and they stand at the foot of my bed, staring at me. I look at the wall.

"The doctor said you're doing well," Dad murmurs. He doesn't know the right words to say right now, I can tell. That's all right, though, because neither do I. There's so much, too much I should be telling them. Things I've wanted to say for a long time—needed to say—but the timing always seemed wrong.

And then I know exactly what to say.

"I'm gay." It drops from my lips like I've said it a hundred times before.

"I'm depressed." It's like I've opened a faucet—everything begins pouring out. "But I'm not depressed because I'm gay. And I'm not depressed because of anything you have or haven't done. It's just an illness. I hope you can accept both of these things about me."

I don't care how old a person is, a son wants his parents to love and accept all parts of him.

My parents both looked surprised, but not nearly as surprised as I thought they'd be. I guess the depression part didn't come as much of a shock at this point.

"Okay," Mom says. "I love you no matter what."

"Same...same for me," Dad husks. "I love you."

"Is this how you really feel? Or are you only taking this so well because I just tried to kill myself?"

I don't know where this is coming from. I guess after facing death—facing what is most people's worst fear, I grew some balls.

"We really feel this way," Mom says gently. "Does the fact that we almost lost you play a part in our acceptance? Maybe. But I know I love you more than anything or anyone on this planet. I'll take you whatever way you come."

I feel like I'm going to puke. Part of me wants to bask in her admission. Another part wants to go back sixty seconds and take back everything I've said. When you live one way for so long, change is difficult.

But I know I need change because what I was doing before obviously wasn't working for me.

"Guy isn't my roommate, he's my boyfriend, and I'm in love with him."

That's everything. They know the worst and the best of me now.

Seventeen

Guy

I stare at the door, my eyes wandering over each line in the grain. I've probably been standing here for close to fifteen minutes. All I have to do is reach out and grab the handle, but I can't make myself do it.

On the other side of the door is my future.

It's been three days since Ian opened his eyes. Three days since I looked at his face or heard his voice.

Too long. Much too long.

But I'm scared of where our relationship is left at this point. I know I need to go inside and find out, but I'm not ready.

The door swings open and I have to step back quickly to avoid being hit. Ian's parents step into the hall and Mrs. Miccoli stops short when she notices me. I shove my hands into my pockets and offer her a polite nod. Before I can comprehend what's happening, she wraps her arms around me, locking my arms to my sides.

"Thank you." She releases me, but cups her palm to my cheek. "For saving my son. And for loving him."

If I had the slightest clue as to how to respond, I still wouldn't be able to.

She takes her husband's hand, and I watch them walk down the hall, completely speechless.

They know.

I don't know how they know, but they clearly do.

The door is standing open, beckoning me into Ian's room, so I finally force myself to go inside. I freeze, my memory warring with my eyes. The last time I saw him, he was pale and haggard looking.

The man sitting in the bed is the man I fell in love with eleven months ago. Blue eyes bright and alert, rosy complexion, and that smile.

God, I missed that smile.

He looks good. He looks so Goddamn good. I almost start sobbing for the twentieth time this week, but this time from nothing but happiness.

"Hi," he breathes.

I nearly stumble to his bed and throw my arms around his neck. His hands fist my shirt at my sides as he takes a shaky breath against my cheek.

"I'm so glad you're okay." I want to say alive—I'm so happy he's alive—but I don't want to remind him of death or how close he came to it, though I'm sure he's thoroughly aware. That's not something he's going to ever forget.

"Me too," he utters.

We hold onto one another, but the silence that settles over us is heavy and uncomfortable. Not the easy, relaxed quiet I'm used to with him.

All the questions are sitting there unasked and all the answers unspoken. Hope told me not to push, so I don't push. Instead, I take a step back so I can look at his face, and I say,

"Do you remember when you tried to teach me how to ice skate?" It's totally random, but for some reason it popped into my head. He bursts out laughing and I suddenly feel choked with so many emotions.

"You fell on your ass more times than I could count," he pants. "It was the funniest shit I've ever witnessed."

"And I dragged you down with me at least half the time."

"Yeah, but I didn't mind you dragging me down with you." He grows quiet again, a far away look clouding his eyes.

"It's one of my favorite days," I continue. "I don't think I ever laughed so hard. I was thinking, this year, we should try it again. You never know, I might actually stay on my feet this time—as long as you hold my hand."

"I'll always hold your hand," he murmurs.

That's the best sentence I've ever heard. I repeat it in my head because it's the polar opposite of how our relationship works. We don't hold hands. Not in public.

"You want to watch TV with me?" He wiggles the remote, smiling invitingly.

"Absolutely." I reach back, pulling the chair over. Ian pats the bed as he moves over, making room for me.

"Lay in bed with me?"

Okay, maybe that's the best sentence I've ever heard. I hesitate—people will see us. He smiles, patting the bed once again.

"I don't give a shit anymore. I want you to lay with me."

I climb into his bed slowly, giving him time to change his mind. He doesn't. Instead, he rests his head on my chest. My hands fold around him instinctively, as if they remember exactly where they belong. And then we stare at the television. I can't tell you what's on or what it's about. My thoughts are consumed with Ian. The way he feels against me, so warm and solid. The sound of his breaths, low and steady. And the fact that he's allowing me to hold him in this public place. It feels like *I'm* the one that's been gone, and now I'm back, exactly where I belong.

I'm home. I'm whole.

I'm happy.

Hours pass this way. The only time we move is when we absolutely have to—but never when a nurse comes in. I know I'll have to leave soon when visiting hours are over, so I try to soak up as much of this as possible now.

I want to ask when he'll be able to come home, but I don't want to push. I opt to keep my mouth busy by placing kisses into his hair. His grip on me tightens and he looks up, his eyes meeting mine. And as if reading my thoughts, he says, "I get to come home Friday."

Best. Sentence. Ever.

My eyes close and I inhale deeply. "I can't wait. I've missed you so much."

"I love you," he whispers for the first time.

My eyes pop open, instantly filling with moisture. That…that is definitely the very best sentence ever uttered.

"I love you too. So much."

Eighteen

Ian

Guy places another *overly cooked* pancake on my plate. It's the least burnt out of the batch. I think he might actually be getting better. I douse it with butter and syrup, trying to mask the taste.

It doesn't work.

I eat it anyway.

In the weeks since I came home from the hospital, things have been really good. Guy and I have started a routine. Healthy breakfast, vitamins, meds, a thirty-minute workout, some "quiet time" as Guy calls it, or as I like to say: My cuddles. This is followed by therapy if we have it that day—twice a week for me and once a week for Guy. Then he goes his way and I go mine until after work.

I know it won't always be this way—this perfect and peaceful—but I can feel myself growing stronger, both mentally and physically. I'll always suffer from anxiety and depression, but the medication, the therapists, and the love and support from my loved ones helps keep me balanced. So when the bad days come, I'll be prepared. And I remind myself every day that the good will always *outweigh* the bad.

And with my Guy, I know we have many, many years to pile on the good.

"I want to try a different workout today," I say around a mouthful of food.

"Okay," Guy says. He smiles at me over his shoulder and I'm flooded with love and desire for this man.

I don't know how I ever got so lucky, but I seriously hit the jackpot with this one.

I set my fork down, walk around the island to where Guy's busy at the stove, and I flip the burner off. He shoots me a quizzical look.

"Well that was rude. I was using that to burn you pancakes."

I shake my head, chuckling. "Come with me. I want to explain the workout."

One light brown eyebrow arches, but he takes my hand, following closely behind me. I tow him into the bedroom where I quickly remove my shirt. My insides are twisting because this is something we haven't done since I've come home. He's hugged me and held me. He's kissed me. But he hasn't made love to me, as if he's afraid I'll break.

"I need you," I murmur.

Guy's Adam's apple bobs in his throat as he watches me strip down. But he doesn't move, frozen solid a foot away.

"Please make love to me."

"Are you sure?"

Am I sure? Maybe he needs some of my crazy meds.

"Hell yes, I'm sure."

I lie back on the bed, watching him. And then I touch myself.

"I've heard a healthy sex life is good for people suffering from depression," Guy says with a smirk.

"You've heard that?" I ask, loving the way that brow pops up once again. His tongue slides over his bottom lip, nearly sending me right over the edge.

He nods. "Orgasms release endorphins. Have you ever been unhappy when you've come?"

"Can't say that I have. But we should test the theory."

"I'm sold." Guy undresses in lightning speed and crawls on top of me. I love this. Us naked, pressed skin to skin.

"What do you want me to do?" he asks softly. "I'll do whatever you want."

"I want you inside of me." I want it so badly I can barely breathe.

He reaches over and opens the side table drawer, removing a condom. Just like our first time together, I take the condom out of his hand and roll it on him. I pump him several times then, making his eyes flutter. He leans into my grasp, enjoying my touch. It makes me feel good that I can do this, that I can give him pleasure.

"I can't wait anymore," I whisper.

"Me neither." He kisses me, his tongue wet and warm against mine. I reach between us and guide him into me. The first few seconds are a mixture of pleasure and pain. And then it's all gratification.

He moves against me slowly, his eyes never leaving mine. I realize in this very instance that the best thing I ever did was fail. If I had succeeded at taking my life, I'd miss out on precious moments like these.

I touch my fingers to Guy's cheek, running my thumb over his lips. "I love you," I say. "Five-ever."

"Five-ever?"

I nod. "Because forever isn't long enough."

He smiles appreciatively down at me. "I love you too. Five-ever and always."

Epilogue

Guy

Ian looks over at me from his chair as the buzzing of the needle begins. I grin at him, reassuringly. He's getting tattoos today. Both of his wrists.

He reaches out with his free hand, connecting it with mine. He squeezes and I'm not sure if it's for comfort or from pain.

Probably a little of both.

"Want to stop at the shelter after this and adopt a dog?" Ian asks out of nowhere.

"A dog?"

He lifts one shoulder in a half shrug. "Or a cat."

"You want pets?"

He nods. "Just one though."

I lift my brows, grinning. "I like animals. Let's get a dog."

He beams back at me before letting his head press into the chair. He closes his eyes and gives my hand another squeeze.

We've come a long way, Ian and I. It's been a bumpy road, but looking back now, I don't think I'd change any of it, even the bad.

I may not have my mom in my life, but I have the unconditional love and support of my friends and family—and now Ian's family. And that's more than enough. I've had a lot of ups and a lot of downs in my life. A lot of hurt and a lot of loss.

But sometimes, you just have to let it be.

The past is the past. It's the reason we are who we are today. The reason we are where we are. And I have to say, I'm pretty happy with my life. The future is a blank slate, waiting to be written, and I plan on writing a love story. Or maybe a comic book. Both are pretty awesome.

The tattoo artist moves on to Ian's second tattoo and I switch to holding his other hand, careful not to touch the freshly inked skin. We both stare down at the words scripted there. *Never forget.*

I brush my thumb over the back of his hand, letting him know I think the tattoo is perfect.

"I'll be right back."

Ian opens his mouth, ready to question me, but I don't want him to know what I'm doing. I leave the room and head back up front to talk to one of the other artists working tonight.

"Do you have time to tattoo me? I just want one word, right here." I run my finger over my heart.

~*~

As soon as I'm finished, I find Ian just leaving his room. His head is cast down, admiring his wrists. I love that he can look at them now with a look of joy on his face. I stop in front of him and he nearly runs into me.

"There you are. Where'd you go?"

"Can I tell you in the car?"

"Okay," he agrees, his brows crinkling. I take his hands into mine and check out the finished results.

Never forget and *Never give up*.

Words to live by.

"Looks good."

"Thanks. It feels good."

I intertwine my fingers with his and we walk that way, hand and hand out to the car. Three months ago, he wouldn't have even considered doing this. Now it's our everyday routine.

"Where'd you go?" he asks again as soon as I shut my door.

I think about making a smartass joke, but I'm too excited and nervous to bother. "I...got a tattoo," I say quietly.

"What? Where?" His eyes flick over me, trying to locate it. I lean back into the seat and lift my shirt. I remove the small wrap covering it and wait for his reaction.

His gaze rakes over it languidly, and then he breaks into gorgeous grin. "Five-ever," he breathes.

"Because forever isn't long enough."

Life is too short. There is always a reason to keep going. If you or someone you know is having thoughts of suicide, there is help.

Call 1-800-273-TALK (8255) or log on to http://www.suicidepreventionlifeline.org

Other books by Cheryl McIntyre:

Sometimes Never (Sometimes Never 1)

Blackbird (A Sometimes Never novella)

Before Now (Sometimes Never 2)

Long After (Sometimes Never 3)

Always Forever (Sometimes Never 4)

Getting Dirty (Dirty 1)

Playing Dirty (Dirty 2)

Talking Dirty (Dirty 3)

Fighting Dirty (Dirty 4)

Staying Dirty (Dirty5)

Infinitely (Infinitely 1)

Eternally (Infinitely 2) Coming soon

Dark Calling (Dark Calling 1)

Dark Craving (Dark Calling 2) Coming soon

Acknowledgments

This is going to be a really difficult acknowledgements to write. I almost don't want to write it. Saying goodbye to this series is comparable for me to when I sent my youngest off to preschool. So I'll try to keep this short and sweet so I don't ruin my laptop with my tears.

I was so incredibly nervous when I started the Sometimes Never series because I had only written one book prior and it was a young adult paranormal romance. The Sometimes Never series was very different. It dealt with real life problems—issues that have affected people in my life. It hasn't just been my blood, sweat, and tears, and time missed with my family that went into this series. It was life. Reality—raw and honest and gritty—went into each and every one of these books—a piece of myself, my life experiences, and teeny, tiny, little parts of my friends and family. And I regret nothing.

I'd like to thank my family for having my back from day one. They never once doubted me and have been my biggest fan and highest encouragement throughout the whole writing process. I love you all more than I can say.

Thank you to my sister, Tammy, who as I've mentioned before, runs and maintains my website. I wouldn't have a website if it wasn't for you because I don't have a single computer-literate bone in my body. You're also a great cheerleader, insisting I write quicker. I promise, I'm working on it.

Thank you to my sister and editor, Dawn. I wrote four different versions of this story and countless versions of the others in the series, and you didn't bat an eyelash. You took it all in stride each and every time. And on top of that, you always make my books better. I don't tell you nearly enough how much I appreciate you. Thank you for putting up with me. No seriously, thank you. I know that's not an easy thing to do.

I want to thank my mommy for passing on the story-telling gene and for always offering up new ideas. When I told you I was writing, you didn't gasp in shock like I assumed you would. Instead, you asked me what it was about and started discussing possible storylines with me. I'll never forget that. It said you had confidence in me. A confidence I didn't have in myself. I love you with all my heart.

To my honey and our children. I'm sorry I write so much and miss so much time with you. And I thank you from the deepest depth of my heart and soul for encouraging my writing despite all that missed time. You are the best family I could have ever hoped for. I love you more than anything else in the world.

I need to give a great big thank you to my author friends. You've all been so kind and supportive. Sunniva Dee, we won't discuss how many times I've emailed you in tears over a bad review, or again, because I'm certain I suck at the whole writing thing. I'm sure you've lost count by now anyway. But I will thank you for being an incredible friend and author. And this also goes to Beth Michele, L.M. Augustine, Devon Herrara, and so many more than I can list. I love our discussions about everything and nothing at all. You are all so great and I love you all dearly.

To all the book bloggers out there, reading book after book and sharing it with others who love books as much as you all do—THANK YOU. And to the bloggers that have been with me since the very start of the Sometimes Never series: Three Chicks and Their Books, Holly's Hot Reads, Rude Girl Book Blog, Holly's Red Hot Reviews, and Smardy Pants Book Blog, I cannot express how much your excitement over my books, your support of me as an author, and your friendship in general means to me. You ladies are all incredible beyond belief and I love you. Love N. Books, thank you for not only all your ongoing support, but for once again, supplying me with a gorgeous man to put on my cover. And to all other blogs that have read and/or shared my books, thank you. I appreciate all that you do.

Last, but certainly not least, thank you reader. I do what I do for you and would be nothing without you.

About the author

Cheryl McIntyre is the author of the bestselling Sometimes Never series, as well as the Dirty series, Infinitely, and Dark Calling. She calls Ohio home, though she secretly dreams of living somewhere much warmer—preferably near a beach.

You can follow her author page on Facebook where she lives part time. On Goodreads—which is like crack for avid readers. On Twitter, though she has still not yet mastered the art of tweeting. Or on her website.